The GHOST Cat Who SAVED My Life

PAMELA BUTCHART

ILLUSTRATED BY
MONIKA FILIPINA

Barrington Stoke

First published in 2023 in Great Britain by
Barrington Stoke Ltd
18 Walker Street, Edinburgh, EH3 7LP

www.barringtonstoke.co.uk

Text © 2023 Pamela Butchart
Illustrations © 2023 Monika Filipina

A CIP catalogue record for this book is available
from the British Library upon request

ISBN: 978-1-80090-215-2

Printed by Hussar Books, Poland

This book is in a super-readable format for young readers
beginning their independent reading journey.

For Bear.
The best and loudest cat ever.
With all our love x x x

CONTENTS

CHAPTER 1
CATS TO THE RESCUE

Everyone's heard of Lassie.

But just in case you haven't, I'll tell you.

Lassie is this famous dog from a film that came out ages ago. And she was always rescuing people and saving them from DANGER.

Some people think only DOGS can help people. You get guide dogs who help people who can't see and police dogs who can sniff out criminals.

But it isn't only dogs that can help people.

CATS can save people too.

And I know that for a fact because this is the story of the GHOST CAT who saved my life!

CHAPTER 2
THE FLAT UPSTAIRS

My name's Liam and this story all started when me and my friend Sav heard a cat meowing. The cat was meowing OVER and OVER in the flat above Sav's flat.

Sav said that she'd been awake ALL NIGHT because of the meowing.

I asked Sav if she'd ever heard the cat before and she shook her head loads and said, "NEVER."

So we went back to playing our computer game but all I could think about was how LOUD the cat was meowing. Was there something wrong with it?

So I said, "I think we should go and check if that cat's OK."

But Sav shook her head and said, "No, Liam, my mum always says not to bother the old lady upstairs. She said she likes to be left alone."

So that's when I said that this was an EMERGENCY because there might be something wrong with her cat.

Sav thought for a minute and then she said, "OK. Let's do this!"

So we shouted to Sav's mum in the kitchen that we were going down to my flat. But we didn't go down to my flat. We went out into the close and ran UP the stairs and knocked on the old lady's door.

But no one answered.

Then all of a sudden Sav's mum shouted, "Sav! Liam! Are you up there?!"

So we ran back down the stairs to Sav's flat and her mum told us off.

I explained that we were just trying to see if the cat that lived upstairs was OK because we were worried about it.

And that's when Sav's mum got a funny look on her face.

And she said, "Cat? What cat? There's no cat upstairs. Mrs Taylor moved out a week ago. No one lives up there any more."

I looked at Sav and Sav looked at me.

And then Sav said, "But, Mum, I definitely heard a cat up there. It was meowing ALL NIGHT!"

Sav's mum shook her head and said, "Well, Mrs Taylor didn't have a cat. And no one lives up there now. Now come in for your lunch. Time to eat!"

But then Sav said, "Mum, I heard it! I heard a cat up there!"

And that's when Sav's mum said, "Well, no one lives up there, so it must have been a GHOST you heard!"

And I looked at Sav.

And Sav looked at me.

Because we'd just found out that
there was a GHOST CAT upstairs!

CHAPTER 3
THE PLAN

The next day, as soon as I'd had my breakfast, I rushed outside to the big bush in the back green.

When I got there, Sav was waiting for me and she had a big shopping bag in her hand and she told me to sit down and listen to THE PLAN.

So I listened and when Sav was finished I said, "Sav, are you sure?"

And Sav nodded and said, "I'm sure."

The plan was to catch the Ghost Cat in the shopping bag and take it back down to Sav's bedroom so she could look after it and keep it as her GHOST PET.

This is why I asked Sav if she
was sure:

1.   How would we get inside
     Mrs Taylor's old flat?

2.   What would happen if Sav's
     mum heard us walking around
     up there?

3.   How do you catch a Ghost Cat
     with a shopping bag?

So I told Sav all of that. But Sav just grinned and said, "Follow me."

So I did.

We went all the way up to the flat with the Ghost Cat.

Sav pushed all the junk mail off the doormat and then she lifted up the mat and said, "YES!"

And that's when I looked and saw that she had a KEY in her hand, so I

said, "How did you know there was a key under there?"

Sav said that she'd seen someone on TV look under the doormat for a key once.

I looked at Sav and Sav looked at me and then we both took a DEEP BREATH.

Then Sav put the key in the lock and the door opened!

CHAPTER 4

AN ORANGE BLURRY THING

We peeped inside the flat but all we could see was a swirly brown carpet and loads of letters on the floor.

Sav said that she was going to go in and that I should follow her. "Shut the door," Sav said, "so the Ghost Cat doesn't get out."

So I nodded and we went into the empty flat and down the hall into the first room but there was nothing to see except more swirly carpet.

But I forgot all about shutting the door because Sav was already looking around the flat.

Then Sav pointed and said, "This flat's the same as mine, so THAT room must be the room above my bedroom. That's where the noise comes from. So that's where the Ghost Cat lives."

We crept inside the room. And my heart was thudding because we were in a room with a Ghost Cat.

Sav opened the shopping bag up
and whispered, "Where is it? Can you
see it?"

But I just shook my head because
I couldn't see anything except old
floorboards and some flowery
wallpaper.

Then all of a sudden Sav shut her eyes and started to wave her arms all over the place.

I didn't know what she was doing but then she said that I needed to close my eyes too. The only way to find a Ghost Cat was to FEEL IT.

So I shut my eyes and copied what Sav was doing, and that's when it happened.

We heard a Ghost Cat MEOW!

We both opened our eyes right away but we still couldn't see or feel anything!

The Ghost Cat kept meowing, over and over, and that's when Sav dropped down to the floor and said, "It's coming from down here somewhere. We need to follow the sound!"

So I got down on the floor too and crawled across the room, and then I worked it out.

The sound was coming from UNDERNEATH us.

I put my ear down to the floor
and that's when I knew the sound was
definitely coming from under the floor!

So I said, "I think the Ghost Cat's
under the floor. It might be trapped!"

And that's when I saw that one of the floorboards was sticking up a bit, so I pulled it out and an ORANGE BLURRY THING leaped out and WHIZZED past us!

Sav rushed after it but when we got to the hall we saw that I'd left the front door open by mistake.

And that the Ghost Cat was GONE.

CHAPTER 5
THE SEARCH

We looked EVERYWHERE for the Ghost Cat.

We even knocked on scary Mrs Kelp's door and asked if she'd seen an orange blurry thing.

But the Ghost Cat was nowhere at all.

Sav sat down on the steps in the landing. And she looked a bit like she was going to cry.

And I knew that it was because she REALLY wanted a pet cat but she couldn't have one because her mum is allergic to cats.

Then Sav said, "The Ghost Cat was my only chance to have a cat. Mum wouldn't have even known it was there! And I don't think ghost cats even HAVE hair!"

I felt TERRIBLE because I knew that if I'd shut the front door, then the Ghost Cat wouldn't have got away. It would have lived in Sav's room and she'd have given it lots of cuddles and love.

So that's when I decided that we weren't giving up.

Because there was ONE place that we hadn't looked.

And I REALLY didn't want to go in there.

But I knew that I HAD to.

So that's when I said, "Stay here. I'll be back!"

CHAPTER 6
TRAPPED IN THE BIN ROOM

When I opened the door to the bin room, the smell was so bad that I thought I was going to be sick.

I knew that I wasn't allowed to go into the bin room but that was the only place that we hadn't looked.

And I also knew that I HAD to find the Ghost Cat. Because Sav is my best friend and this was the only chance she'd ever get to have a pet cat.

I made sure that the big brick was in place to keep the bin-room door open – it's there to make sure fresh air can come in. And then I got down on my hands and knees and started looking for the Ghost Cat under the big bins.

Suddenly, I heard a noise at the door. But when I looked up there was nothing there.

I went back to looking under the bins for the Ghost Cat and that's when I heard another noise and it was coming from INSIDE one of the big bins that everyone throws their rubbish into.

I climbed up the side but I couldn't see anything.

So I climbed up a bit more and leaned over and that's when I saw an ORANGE GHOST CAT TAIL.

But then I slipped, and as I fell, the cat leaped out and ZOOMED out of the room.

I lay on the floor and my back hurt.
So did my head.

I got up as fast as I could to follow
the Ghost Cat. But it was too late
because I had knocked the brick to
one side and the door of the bin room
was SHUT.

I looked for a handle so I could open it but there wasn't one. And that's when I knew that the REAL reason for the big brick to stop the door from closing was because the door doesn't open from the inside.

It was DARK inside the bin room and I couldn't find a light switch anywhere.

I banged on the door for AGES and shouted, "HELP! I'M STUCK!"

But no one came. And I knew that it was because the door was solid and that no one in the close could hear me.

I sat on the floor and waited and waited for AGES.

I tried not to panic but that was hard because my tummy was rumbling and I'd missed my lunch and maybe even my tea and I was starting to think that no one was going to find me for DAYS and that I was going to STARVE TO DEATH.

CHAPTER 7
THE RESCUE!

I must have fallen asleep because the next thing I remember is someone shaking me and shouting my name!

I opened my eyes and that's when I saw that it was Sav shaking me and that her mum was there too and that the door was open again.

Then my mum came rushing in and she grabbed me and gave me a big hug and she kept asking me over and over if I was OK.

So I said that I was and that the door had shut and I couldn't get out and that I was sorry.

Then Mum said that she had been WORRIED SICK and that I'd been missing ALL MORNING.

So that's when I told Mum that I'd been looking for the Ghost Cat and that I'd seen it in the bin but it had run away and now it was gone.

I looked at Sav and said sorry and that's when she started smiling.

I had no idea why Sav was smiling but then she said, "Look!"

And she pointed to the doorway and that's when I saw a little orange and white cat sitting there watching us.

Then Sav said, "It's not a ghost. It's a REAL cat! And it SAVED YOU!"

I looked at Sav and then at Mum because I didn't understand what Sav was saying.

And that's when Sav explained that the little orange and white cat had been meowing outside everyone's doors in the block and then running away when people answered. And then coming back and doing it again.

Sav said she'd worked out that the cat wanted someone to follow it and that when they did, it led them all the way down to the bin room and scratched at the door until they opened it.

Then Sav said, "Everyone's been looking for you and the Ghost Cat knew where you were all along and was trying to tell us!"

I couldn't believe it. The Ghost Cat had SAVED ME!

I looked over at the little cat. It was TINY.

That's when I said, "It was trapped under the floor upstairs. I think it's starving. It was in the bins looking for food."

And Mum said, "Yes, Sav told us you were in the flat upstairs. You should NOT have been up there!"

And I said sorry.

Then Sav's mum said that the cat must have snuck in when the movers were moving Mrs Taylor out and got trapped under the floor somehow.

Then Sav said, "It doesn't have a collar. And it's all thin. We think it's a stray."

I looked at the cat who saved my life and said, "Hi, Ghost Cat. Thanks for saving me. Are you hungry?"

And that's when the little cat meowed.

And then it walked right over and sat on my knee!

I looked up at Sav and she looked just as shocked as I was!

Then Sav sat down on the ground and
put her legs together and said, "Here,
Ghostie. Come see me too, Ghostie."

And then the cat jumped off my legs
and curled up on Sav's lap and started to
purr loads.

Sav looked up at her mum and said, "Mum. PLEASE can we keep the Ghost Cat? PLEASE."

But Sav's mum shook her head and said that she was allergic and that she was going to call the SSPCA to come and take the cat away.

And that's when I had an idea.

So I looked up at Mum and said,
"Can we keep it? I mean, can we keep
it FOR Sav? It can live at our house but
it'll be Sav's cat. And maybe a little bit
my cat too? Please?"

My mum looked at me and then at
Sav and then at the cat but she didn't
say anything.

But I knew that she was thinking about it because Mum LOVES cats.

We had a cat when I was a baby and I know that Mum misses it because she still keeps its collar and its favourite toy in a little box by her bed.

So that's when Mum made me promise that I would NEVER go into the bin room again. And that I would NEVER go into an empty flat or ANY flat without asking her first. And I nodded loads and said that I wouldn't and I meant it.

Then Mum said I also had to do ALL the washing-up AND the drying for a MONTH because I'd broken the rules. And I nodded even more because I knew what she was about to say.

And that's when Mum said, "OK. We can keep her."

I looked at Sav and Sav was actually crying. But I knew that they were happy tears.

I leaned forward and gave the cat a little tickle under her chin and said, "Welcome home, Ghostie! Thanks for saving me."

And the cat did a REALLY LOUD meow and Mum said, "I hope she's not as loud as that all the time!"

And I looked at Sav and we both burst out laughing because we knew that the Ghost Cat WAS a loud cat.

But I knew that it was a good thing that Ghostie was a loud cat.

Because her loud meow had saved her.

And it had saved me too!